LoVe MonsteR
and the Perfect Present

Rachel Bright

WELCOME TO
CUTESVILLE
Home of the fluffy

and slightly hairy

SCHOLASTIC INC.

This mOnster...

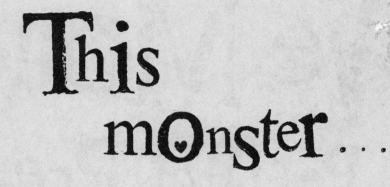

(HellO, LOVe MonSter.)

thinks THIS mOnster . . .

is the most perfect
mOnster in the World.

Yes, they are the **bestest** of friends.

They spend each and every day together.
Sometimes doing fun stuff outside.

Sometimes doing fun stuff inside.

And sometimes . . .

doing nothing at all.

But there is **one day** in Cutesville, where these particular m**o**nsters live, that is different from **all** the others.

CUTESVILLE ANNU

DAY BEFORE YESTERDAY
outside

DAY BEFORE THE DAY BEFORE YESTERDAY
inside

DAY AFTER SPECIAL DAY
Rel

AGES AGO
can't remember

SPECIAL DAY
* LIKE NO OTHER *

AGES AG

NEXT DAY, get excited with whole town

AGES + AGES AWAY

AGES AWAY

CALENDAR
TOMORROW
decorate Cutesville with lights
TODAY
plan music for special day
DAY
nothing together
AGES AWAY
outside
AGES AWAY
plan rest of year
plan ↗
DAY AFTER THE DAY AFTER SPECIAL DAY
play outside
THE FUTURE
← Silver Clothes (otherwise the same)
ONE DAY
go to moon
ONE DAY SOON
skipping
ES+
AY
Dentist

A **VERY** special day, in fact,
when the streets are filled with lights,
the air is filled with music . . .

and the whole town gets **SUPER** excited.

Yes, once a year in Cutesville it's . . .

PRESENT DAY

when everyone gives
a lovely someone
something lovely...

- OH MY -
- GOODNESS -

to show how special they are.

It's pretty much the best day ever.

So why does this monster look so worried?

But finding such a thing is **not easy**.

Hmmmm. It was time to think very hard
and to...

And, oh! The shops were FULL OF HUNDREDS OF WONDERFUL, SHINYFUL things!

Love Monster was SURE
he'd come to the right place!

But as it turned out,
wonderful, shinyful things...

Can be expensive.
VERY expensive indeed.

There just wasn't enough in his saving-up jar.
Oh dear. Poor monster.

What WAS he to do?
It was almost Present Day, and there
was only one thing worse than a
not-perfect present...

and that was
NO PRESENT
AT ALL!

Love Monster worried
all the way home.

END OF THE ROAD GIFTS

LAST CHANCE

WOO-HOO! PRESENT DAY TOMORROW!

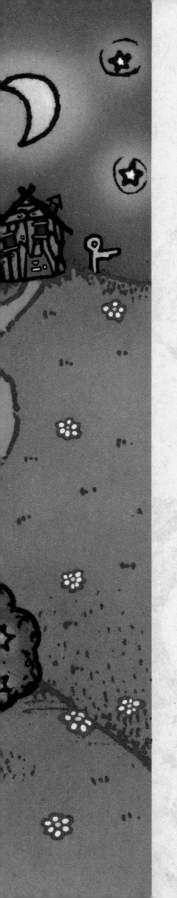

He had NOTHING!

NOTHING to show his
perfect monster how much he cared.

STUFF TO DO OUTSI...

BUYING PRESENT...

NON-CUT...

STUFF TO DO INSIDE

BAKING

PERFECT THINGS

PERFECT Things to MAKE & DO for that special someone

But that was when it hit him:

BOINK

Perhaps he had
EVERYTHING he needed!

He had paints and glitter.

He had some
Wood and
some glue.

And, most important of all,
he had AN IDEA!

There was
A LOT
to do.

And
not a lot
of time
to do it.

He worked
all night,

until the sun
came up.

And when
Present Day
arrived . . .

so did the most perfect
monster in the world.

And, phew!
Love Monster DID
have something to give.

Something to be very proud of.

You see, sometimes the perfect present doesn't have to cost very much...

to mean absolutely everything.

For my parents, for the gift of life & unconditional love,
my monster, for the gift of us,
& Anna & Ali, for friendship & good times.

Also with special thank-yous to my sister, for her help,
& to Mandy & Helen, for the gift of belief.

First published in Great Britain by HarperCollins Children's Books in 2013

ISBN 978-0-545-92756-7

12 11 10 9 8 7 6 5 4 3 2 1   15 16 17 18 19 20/0

Printed in the U.S.A.   08

First Scholastic printing, November 2015

Designed by Kristie Radwilowicz